THE HAUNTED MOUNTAIN

BY

ROBERT E. HOWARD

British Library Cataloguing-in-Publication Data
A catalogue record for this book is available from the
British Library

Robert E. Howard

Robert Ervin Howard was born in Peaster, Texas in 1906. During his youth, his family moved between a variety of Texan boomtowns, and Howard – a bookish and somewhat introverted child – was steeped in the violent myths and legends of the Old South. Although he loved reading and learning, Howard developed a distinctly Texan, hardboiled outlook on the world. He became a passionate fan of boxing, taking it up at an amateur level, and from the age of nine began to write adventure tales of semi-historical bloodshed. In 1919, when Howard was thirteen, his family moved to the Central Texas hamlet of Cross Plains, where he would stay for the rest of his life.

At fifteen Howard began to read the pulp magazines of the day, and to write more seriously. The December 1922 issue of his high school newspaper featured two of his stories, 'Golden Hope Christmas' and 'West is West'. In 1924 he sold his first piece – a short caveman tale titled 'Spear and Fang' – for $16 to the not-yet-famous *Weird Tales* magazine. He published with the magazine regularly over the next few years. 1929 was a breakout year for Howard, in that the 23-year-old writer began to sell to other magazines, such as *Ghost Stories* and *Argosy,* both of whom had previously sent him hundreds of rejection slips. In 1930, he began a correspondence with weird fiction master H. P. Lovecraft which ran up to his death six years later, and is regarded as one of the great correspondence cycles in all of fantasy literature.

It was partly due to Lovecraft's encouragement that Howard created his most famous character, Conan the Cimmerian. Conan – a barbarian-turned-King during the Hyborian Age, a mythical period of some 12,000 years ago – featured in seventeen *Weird Tales* stories between 1933 and 1936, and is now regarded as having spawned the 'sword and sorcery' genre, making Howard's influence on fantasy literature comparable to that of J. R. R. Tolkien's. The Conan stories have since been adapted many times, most famously in the series of films starring Arnold Schwarzenegger.

Howard was enjoying an all-time high in sales by the beginning of 1936, but he was also deeply upset by the ill health of his mother, who had fallen into a coma. On the morning of June 11, 1936, he asked an attending nurse whether she would ever recover, and the nurse replied negatively. Howard walked to his car, parked outside the family home in Cross Plains, and shot himself. He died eight hours later, aged just thirty.

The reason I despises tarantulas, stinging lizards, and hydrophobia skunks is because they reminds me so much of Aunt Lavaca, which my Uncle Jacob Grimes married in a absent-minded moment, when he was old enough to know better.

That-there woman's voice plumb puts my teeth on aidge, and it has the same effect on my horse, Cap'n Kidd, which don't generally shy at nothing less'n a rattlesnake. So when she stuck her head out of her cabin as I was riding by and yelled "Breckinri-i-idge," Cap'n Kidd jumped straight up in the air, and then tried to buck me off.

"Stop tormentin' that pore animal and come here," Aunt Lavaca commanded, whilst I was fighting for my life against Cap'n Kidd's spine-twisting sun-fishing. "I never see such a cruel, worthless, no-good--"

She kept right on yapping away until I finally wore him down and reined up alongside the cabin stoop and said: "What you want, Aunt Lavaca?"

She give me a scornful snort, and put her hands onto her hips and glared at me like I was something she didn't like the smell of.

"I want you should go git yore Uncle Jacob and bring him home," she said at last. "He's off on one of his idiotic prospectin' sprees again. He snuck out before daylight with the bay mare and a pack mule--I wisht I'd woke up and caught him. I'd of fixed him! If you hustle you can catch him this side of Haunted Mountain Gap. You bring him back if you have to lasso him and tie him to his saddle. Old fool! Off huntin' gold when they's work to be did in the alfalfa fields. Says he ain't no farmer. Huh! I 'low I'll make a farmer outa him yet. You git goin'."

"But I ain't got time to go chasin' Uncle Jacob all over Haunted Mountain," I protested. "I'm headin' for the rodeo over to Chawed Ear. I'm goin' to win me a prize bull-doggin' some steers--"

"Bull-doggin'!" she snapped. "A fine ockerpashun! Gwan, you worthless loafer! I ain't goin' to stand here all day argyin' with a big ninny like you be. Of all the good-for-nothin', triflin', lunkheaded--"

When Aunt Lavaca starts in like that you might as well travel. She can talk steady for three days and nights without repeating herself, her voice getting louder and shriller all the time till it nigh splits a body's eardrums. She was still yelling at me as I rode up the trail toward Haunted Mountain Gap, and I could hear her long after I couldn't see her no more.

Pore Uncle Jacob! He never had much luck prospecting, but trailing around through the mountains with a jackass is a lot better'n listening to Aunt Lavaca. A jackass's voice is mild and soothing alongside of hers.

Some hours later I was climbing the long rise that led up to the Gap, and I realized I had overtook the old coot when something went ping! up on the slope, and my hat flew off. I quick reined Cap'n Kidd behind a clump of bresh, and looked up toward the Gap, and seen a packmule's rear-end sticking out of a cluster of boulders.

"You quit that shootin' at me, Uncle Jacob!" I roared.

"You stay whar you be," his voice come back, sharp as a razor. "I know Lavacky sent you after me, but I ain't goin' home. I'm onto somethin' big at last, and I don't aim to be interfered with."

"What you mean?" I demanded.

"Keep back or I'll ventilate you," he promised. "I'm goin' for the Lost Haunted Mine."

"You been huntin' that thing for thirty years," I snorted.

"This time I finds it," he says. "I bought a map off'n a drunk Mex down to Perdition. One of his ancestors was a Injun which helped pile up the rocks to hide the mouth of the cave where it is."

"Why didn't he go find it and git the gold?" I asked.

"He's skeered of ghosts," said Uncle Jacob. "All Mexes is awful superstitious. This-un 'ud ruther set and drink, nohow. They's millions in gold in that-there mine. I'll shoot you before I'll go home. Now will you go on back peaceable, or will you throw-in with me? I might need you, in case the pack mule plays out."

"I'll come with you," I said, impressed. "Maybe you have got somethin', at that. Put up yore Winchester. I'm comin'."

He emerged from his rocks, a skinny leathery old cuss, and he said: "What about Lavacky? If you don't come back with me, she'll foller us herself. She's that strong-minded."

"I'll leave a note for her," I said. "Joe Hopkins always comes down through the Gap onct a week on his way to Chawed Ear. He's due through here today. I'll stick the note on a tree, where he'll see it and take it to her."

I had a pencil-stub in my saddle-bag, and I tore a piece of wrapping paper off'n a can of tomaters Uncle Jacob had in his pack, and I writ:

Dere Ant Lavaca:

I am takin uncle Jacob way up in the mountins dont try to foler us it wont do no good gold is what Im after. Breckinridge.

I folded it and writ on the outside:

Dere Joe: pleeze take this here note to Miz Lavaca Grimes on the Chawed Ear rode.

THEN ME AND UNCLE JACOB sot out for the higher ranges, and he started telling me all about the Lost Haunted Mine again, like he'd already did about forty times before. Seems like they was onct a old prospector which stumbled onto a cave about fifty years before then, which the walls was solid gold and nuggets all over the floor till a

6

body couldn't walk, as big as mushmelons. But the Indians jumped him and run him out and he got lost and nearly starved in the desert, and went crazy. When he come to a settlement and finally regained his mind, he tried to lead a party back to it, but never could find it. Uncle Jacob said the Indians had took rocks and bresh and hid the mouth of the cave so nobody could tell it was there. I asked him how he knowed the Indians done that, and he said it was common knowledge. Any fool oughta know that's just what they done.

"This-here mine," says Uncle Jacob, "is located in a hidden valley which lies away up amongst the high ranges. I ain't never seen it, and I thought I'd explored these mountains plenty. Ain't nobody more familiar with 'em than me except old Joshua Braxton. But it stands to reason that the cave is awful hard to find, or somebody'd already found it. Accordin' to this-here map, that lost valley must lie just beyond Apache Canyon. Ain't many white men knows whar that is, even. We're headin' there."

We had left the Gap far behind us, and was moving along the slanting side of a sharp-angled crag whilst he was talking. As we passed it, we seen two figgers with horses emerge from the other side, heading in the same direction we was, so our trails converged. Uncle Jacob glared and reached for his Winchester.

"Who's that?" he snarled.

"The big un's Bill Glanton," I said. "I never seen t'other'n."

"And nobody else, outside of a freak museum," growled Uncle Jacob.

This other feller was a funny-looking little maverick, with laced boots and a cork sun-helmet and big spectacles. He sot his horse like he thought it was a rocking chair, and held his reins like he was trying to fish with 'em. Glanton hailed us. He was from Texas, original, and was rough in his speech and free with his weapons, but me and him had always got along very well.

"Where you-all goin'?" demanded Uncle Jacob.

"I am Professor Van Brock, of New York," said the tenderfoot, whilst Bill was getting rid of his tobaccer wad. "I have employed Mr. Glanton, here, to guide me up into the mountains. I am on the track of a tribe of aborigines, which, according to fairly well substantiated rumor, have inhabited the Haunted Mountains since time immemorial."

"Lissen here, you four-eyed runt," said Uncle Jacob in wrath, "are you givin' me the horse-laugh?"

"I assure you that equine levity is the furthest thing from my thoughts," says Van Brock. "Whilst touring the country in the interests of science, I heard the rumors to which I have referred. In a village possessing the singular appellation of Chawed Ear, I met an aged prospector who told me that he had seen one of the aborigines, clad in the skin of a wild

8

animal and armed with a bludgeon. The wildman, he said, emitted a most peculiar and piercing cry when sighted, and fled into the recesses of the hills. I am confident that it is some survivor of a pre-Indian race, and I am determined to investigate."

"They ain't no such critter in these hills," snorted Uncle Jacob. "I've roamed all over 'em for thirty year, and I ain't seen no wildman."

"Well," says Glanton, "they's somethin' onnatural up there, because I been hearin' some funny yarns myself. I never thought I'd be huntin' wildmen," he says, "but since that hash-slinger in Perdition turned me down to elope with a travelin' salesman, I welcomes the chance to lose myself in the mountains and forgit the perfidy of women-kind. What you-all doin' up here? Prospectin'?" he said, glancing at the tools on the mule.

"Not in earnest," said Uncle Jacob hurriedly. "We're just kinda whilin' away our time. They ain't no gold in these mountains."

"Folks says that Lost Haunted Mine is up here somewhere," said Glanton.

"A pack of lies," snorted Uncle Jacob, busting into a sweat. "Ain't no such mine. Well, Breckinridge, let's be shovin'. Got to make Antelope Peak before sundown."

"I thought we was goin' to Apache Canyon," I says, and he give me a awful glare, and said: "Yes, Breckinridge, that's right, Antelope Peak, just like you said. So long, gents."

"So long," said Glanton.

So we turned off the trail almost at right-angles to our course, me follering Uncle Jacob bewilderedly. When we was out of sight of the others, he reined around again.

"When Nature give you the body of a giant, Breckinridge," he said, "she plumb forgot to give you any brains to go along with yore muscles. You want everybody to know what we're lookin' for?"

"Aw," I said, "them fellers is just lookin' for wildmen."

"Wildmen!" he snorted. "They don't have to go no further'n Chawed Ear on payday night to find more wildmen than they could handle. I ain't swallerin' no such stuff. Gold is what they're after, I tell you. I seen Glanton talkin' to that Mex in Perdition the day I bought that map from him. I believe they either got wind of that mine, or know I got that map, or both."

"What you goin' to do?" I asked him.

"Head for Apache Canyon by another trail," he said.

SO WE DONE SO AND ARRIV there after night, him not willing to stop till we got there. It was deep, with big high cliffs cut with ravines and gulches here and there, and very wild in appearance. We didn't descend into the canyon that night, but camped on a plateau above it. Uncle

Jacob 'lowed we'd begin exploring next morning. He said they was lots of caves in the canyon, and he'd been in all of 'em. He said he hadn't never found nothing except b'ars and painters and rattlesnakes; but he believed one of them caves went on through into another, hidden canyon, and there was where the gold was at.

Next morning I was awoke by Uncle Jacob shaking me, and his whiskers was curling with rage.

"What's the matter?" I demanded, setting up and pulling my guns.

"They're here!" he squalled. "Daw-gone it, I suspected 'em all the time! Git up, you big lunk. Don't set there gawpin' with a gun in each hand like a idjit! They're here, I tell you!"

"Who's here?" I asked.

"That dern tenderfoot and his cussed Texas gunfighter," snarled Uncle Jacob. "I was up just at daylight, and purty soon I seen a wisp of smoke curlin' up from behind a big rock t'other side of the flat. I snuck over there, and there was Glanton fryin' bacon, and Van Brock was pertendin' to be lookin' at some flowers with a magnifyin' glass--the blame fake. He ain't no perfessor. I bet he's a derned crook. They're follerin' us. They aim to murder us and rob us of my map."

"Aw, Glanton wouldn't do that," I said. And Uncle Jacob said: "You shet up! A man will do anything whar gold is consarned. Dang it all, git up and do somethin'! Air you goin' to set there, you big lummox, and let us git murdered in our sleep?"

That's the trouble of being the biggest man in yore clan; the rest of the family always dumps all the onpleasant jobs onto yore shoulders. I pulled on my boots and headed across the flat, with Uncle Jacob's war-songs ringing in my ears, and I didn't notice whether he was bringing up the rear with his Winchester or not.

They was a scattering of trees on the flat, and about halfway across a figger emerged from amongst them, headed my direction with fire in his eye. It was Glanton.

"So, you big mountain grizzly," he greeted me rambunctiously, "you was goin' to Antelope Peak, hey? Kinda got off the road, didn't you? Oh, we're on to you, we are!"

"What you mean?" I demanded. He was acting like he was the one which oughta feel righteously indignant, instead of me.

"You know what I mean!" he says, frothing slightly at the mouth. "I didn't believe it when Van Brock first said he suspicioned you, even though you hombres did act funny yesterday when we met you on the trail. But this mornin' when I glimpsed yore fool Uncle Jacob spyin' on our camp, and then seen him sneakin' off through the bresh, I knowed Van Brock was right. Yo're after what we're after, and you-all resorts to dirty onderhanded tactics. Does you deny yo're after the same thing we are?"

"Naw, I don't," I said. "Uncle Jacob's got more right to it than you-all. And when you says we uses underhanded tricks, yo're a liar."

"That settles it!" gnashed he. "Go for yore gun!"

"I don't want to perforate you," I growled.

"I ain't hankerin' to conclude yore mortal career," he admitted. "But Haunted Mountain ain't big enough for both of us. Take off yore guns and I'll maul the livin' daylights outa you, big as you be."

I unbuckled my gun-belt and hung it on a limb, and he laid off his'n, and hit me in the stummick and on the ear and in the nose, and then he socked me in the jaw and knocked out a tooth. This made me mad, so I taken him by the neck and threw him against the ground so hard it jolted all the wind outa him. I then sot on him and started banging his head against a convenient boulder, and his cussing was terrible to hear.

"If you all had acted like white men," I gritted, "we'd of give you a share in that there mine."

"What you talkin' about?" he gurgled, trying to haul his bowie out of his boot which I had my knee on.

"The Lost Haunted Mine, of course," I snarled, getting a fresh grip on his ears.

"Hold on," he protested. "You mean you-all are just lookin' for gold? On the level?"

13

I was so astonished I quit hammering his skull against the rock.

"Why, what else?" I demanded. "Ain't you-all follerin' us to steal Uncle Jacob's map which shows where at the mine is hid?"

"Git offa me," he snorted disgustfully, taking advantage of my surprize to push me off. "Hell!" he said, starting to knock the dust offa his britches. "I might of knowed that tenderfoot was wool-gatherin'. After we seen you-all yesterday, and he heard you mention 'Apache Canyon' he told me he believed you was follerin' us. He said that yarn about prospectin' was just a blind. He said he believed you was workin' for a rival scientific society to git ahead of us and capture that-there wildman yoreselves."

"What?" I said. "You mean that wildman yarn is straight?"

"So far as we're consarned," said Bill. "Prospectors is been tellin' some onusual stories about Apache Canyon. Well, I laughed at him at first, but he kept on usin' so many .45-caliber words that he got me to believin' it might be so. 'Cause, after all, here was me guidin' a tenderfoot on the trail of a wildman, and they wasn't no reason to think you and Jacob Grimes was any more sensible than me.

"Then, this mornin' when I seen Joab peekin' at me from the bresh, I decided Van Brock must be right. You-all hadn't never went to Antelope Peak. The more I thought it over, the more sartain I was that you was follerin' us to steal our wildman, so I started over to have a showdown."

"Well," I said, "we've reached a understandin' at last. You don't want our mine, and we shore don't want yore wildman. They's plenty of them amongst my relatives on Bear Creek. Le's git Van Brock and lug him over to our camp and explain things to him and my weak-minded uncle."

"All right," said Glanton, buckling on his guns. "Hey, what's that?"

From down in the canyon come a yell: "Help! Aid! Assistance!"

"It's Van Brock!" yelped Glanton. "He's wandered down into the canyon by hisself! Come on!"

RIGHT NEAR THEIR CAMP they was a ravine leading down to the floor of the canyon. We pelted down that at full speed, and emerged near the wall of the cliffs. They was the black mouth of a cave showing nearby, in a kind of cleft, and just outside this cleft Van Brock was staggering around, yowling like a hound dawg with his tail caught in the door.

His cork helmet was laying on the ground all bashed outa shape, and his specs was lying near it. He had a knob on his head as big as a turnip and he was doing a kind of ghost-dance or something all over the place.

He couldn't see very good without his specs, 'cause when he sighted us he give a shriek and starting legging it

15

for the other end of the canyon, seeming to think we was more enemies. Not wanting to indulge in no sprint in that heat, Bill shot a heel offa his boot, and that brung him down squalling blue murder.

"Help!" he shrieked. "Mr. Glanton! Help! I am being attacked! Help!"

"Aw, shet up," snorted Bill. "I'm Glanton. Yo're all right. Give him his specs, Breck. Now what's the matter?"

He put 'em on, gasping for breath, and staggered up, wild-eyed, and p'inted at the cave and hollered: "The wildman! I saw him, as I descended into the canyon on a private exploring expedition! A giant with a panther-skin about his waist, and a club in his hand. He dealt me a murderous blow with the bludgeon when I sought to apprehend him, and fled into that cavern. He should be arrested!"

I looked into the cave. It was too dark to see anything except for a hoot-owl.

"He must of saw somethin', Breck," said Glanton, hitching his gun-harness. "Somethin' shore cracked him on the conk. I've been hearin' some queer tales about this canyon, myself. Maybe I better sling some lead in there--"

"No, no, no!" broke in Van Brock. "We must capture him alive!"

"What's goin' on here?" said a voice, and we turned to see Uncle Jacob approaching with his Winchester in his hands.

"Everything's all right, Uncle Jacob," I said. "They don't want yore mine. They're after the wildman, like they said, and we got him cornered in that there cave."

"All right, huh?" he snorted. "I reckon you thinks it's all right for you to waste yore time with such dern foolishness when you oughta be helpin' me look for my mine. A big help you be!"

"Where was you whilst I was argyin' with Bill here?" I demanded.

"I knowed you could handle the sityation, so I started explorin' the canyon," he said. "Come on, we got work to do."

"But the wildman!" cried Van Brock. "Your nephew would be invaluable in securing the specimen. Think of science! Think of progress! Think of--"

"Think of a striped skunk!" snorted Uncle Jacob. "Breckinridge, air you comin'?"

"Aw, shet up," I said disgustedly. "You both make me tired. I'm goin' in there and run that wildman out, and Bill, you shoot him in the hind-laig as he comes out, so's we can catch him and tie him up."

"But you left yore guns hangin' onto that limb up on the plateau," objected Glanton.

"I don't need 'em," I said. "Didn't you hear Van Brock say we was to catch him alive? If I started shootin' in the dark I might rooin him."

"All right," says Bill, cocking his six-shooters. "Go ahead. I figger yo're a match for any wildman that ever come down the pike."

So I went into the cleft and entered the cave, and it was dark as all get-out. I groped my way along and discovered the main tunnel split into two, so I taken the biggest one. It seemed to get darker the further I went, and purty soon I bumped into something big and hairy and it went "Wump!" and grabbed me.

Thinks I, it's the wildman, and he's on the war-path. We waded into each other and tumbled around on the rocky floor in the dark, biting and mauling and tearing. I'm the biggest and the fightingest man on Bear Creek, which is famed far and wide for its ring-tailed scrappers, but this wildman shore give me my hands full. He was the biggest hairiest critter I ever laid hands on, and be had more teeth and talons than I thought a human could possibly have. He chawed me with vigor and enthusiasm, and he waltzed up and down my frame free and hearty, and swept the floor with me till I was groggy.

For a while I thought I was going to give up the ghost, and I thought with despair of how humiliated my relatives on Bear Creek would be to hear their champion battler had been clawed to death by a wildman in a cave.

That made me plumb ashamed for weakening, and the socks I give him ought to of laid out any man, wild or tame, to say nothing of the pile-driver kicks in his belly, and butting him with my head so he gasped. I got what felt like a ear in my mouth and commenced chawing on it, and presently, what with this and other mayhem I committed on him, he give a most inhuman squall and bust away and went lickety-split for the outside world.

I riz up and staggered after him, hearing a wild chorus of yells break forth outside, but no shots. I bust out into the open, bloody all over, and my clothes hanging in tatters.

"Where is he?" I hollered. "Did you let him git away?"

"Who?" said Glanton, coming out from behind a boulder, whilst Van Brock and Uncle Jacob dropped down out of a tree nearby.

"The wildman, damn it!" I roared.

"We ain't seen no wildman," said Glanton.

"Well, what was that thing I just run outa the cave?" I hollered.

"That was a grizzly b'ar," said Glanton. "Yeah," sneered Uncle Jacob, "and that was Van Brock's 'wildman'! And now, Breckinridge, if yo're through playin', we'll--"

"No, no!" hollered Van Brock, jumping up and down. "It was a human being which smote me and fled into the cavern. Not a bear! It is still in there somewhere, unless there is another exit to the cavern."

"Well, he ain't in there now," said Uncle Jacob, peering into the mouth of the cave. "Not even a wildman would

19

run into a grizzly's cave, or if he did, he wouldn't stay long-
-ooomp!"

A rock come whizzing out of the cave and hit Uncle
Jacob in the belly, and he doubled up on the ground.

"Aha!" I roared, knocking up Glanton's ready six-
shooter. "I know! They's two tunnels in here. He's in that
smaller cave. I went into the wrong one! Stay here, you-all,
and gimme room! This time I gets him!"

WITH THAT I RUSHED INTO the cave mouth
again, disregarding some more rocks which emerged, and
plunged into the smaller opening. It was dark as pitch, but
I seemed to be running along a narrer tunnel, and ahead of
me I heered bare feet pattering on the rock. I follered 'em at
full lope, and presently seen a faint hint of light. The next
minute I rounded a turn and come out into a wide place,
which was lit by a shaft of light coming in through a cleft in
the wall, some yards up. In the light I seen a fantastic figger
climbing up on a ledge, trying to reach that cleft.

"Come down offa that!" I thundered, and give a leap
and grabbed the ledge by one hand and hung on, and reached
for his legs with t'other hand. He give a squall as I grabbed
his ankle and splintered his club over my head. The force
of the lick broke off the lip of the rock ledge I was holding
to, and we crashed to the floor together, because I didn't
let loose of him. Fortunately, I hit the rock floor headfirst
which broke my fall and kept me from fracturing any of my

important limbs, and his head hit my jaw, which rendered him unconscious.

I riz up and picked up my limp captive and carried him out into the daylight where the others was waiting. I dumped him on the ground and they stared at him like they couldn't believe it. He was a ga'nt old cuss with whiskers about a foot long and matted hair, and he had a mountain lion's hide tied around his waist.

"A white man!" enthused Van Brock, dancing up and down. "An unmistakable Caucasian! This is stupendous! A prehistoric survivor of a pre-Indian epoch! What an aid to anthropology! A wildman! A veritable wildman!"

"Wildman, hell!" snorted Uncle Jacob. "That-there's old Joshua Braxton, which was tryin' to marry that old maid schoolteacher down at Chawed Ear all last winter."

"I was tryin' to marry her!" said Joshua bitterly, setting up suddenly and glaring at all of us. "That-there is good, that-there is! And me all the time fightin' for my life against it. Her and all her relations was tryin' to marry her to me. They made my life a curse. They was finally all set to kidnap me and marry me by force. That's why I come away off up here, and put on this rig to scare folks away. All I craves is peace and quiet and no dern women."

Van Brock begun to cry because they wasn't no wildman, and Uncle Jacob said: "Well, now that this dern foolishness is settled, maybe I can git to somethin' important. Joshua, you know these mountains even better'n I do. I want you to help me find the Lost Haunted Mine."

"There ain't no such mine," said Joshua. "That old prospector imagined all that stuff whilst he was wanderin' around over the desert crazy."

"But I got a map I bought from a Mexican in Perdition," hollered Uncle Jacob.

"Lemme see that map," said Glanton. "Why, hell," he said, "that-there is a fake. I seen that Mexican drawin' it, and he said he was goin' to try to sell it to some old jassack for the price of a drunk."

Uncle Jacob sot down on a rock and pulled his whiskers. "My dreams is bust," he said weakly. "I'm goin' home to my wife."

"You must be desperate if it's come to that," said old Joshua acidly. "You better stay up here. If they ain't no gold, they ain't no women to torment a body, either."

"Women is a snare and a delusion," agreed Glanton. "Van Brock can go back with these fellers. I'm stayin' with Joshua."

"You-all oughta be ashamed talkin' about women that way," I reproached 'em. "What, in this here lousy and troubled world can compare to women's gentle sweetness--"

"There the scoundred is!" screeched a familiar voice. "Don't let him git away! Shoot him if he tries to run!"

WE TURNED SUDDEN. We'd been argying so loud amongst ourselves we hadn't noticed a gang of folks coming down the ravine. There was Aunt Lavaca and the sheriff of Chawed Ear with ten men, and they all p'inted sawed-off shotguns at me.

"Don't get rough, Elkins," warned the sheriff nervously. "They're all loaded with buckshot and ten-penny nails. I knows yore repertation and I takes no chances. I arrests you for the kidnapin' of Jacob Grimes."

"Are you plumb crazy?" I demanded.

"Kidnapin'!" hollered Aunt Lavaca, waving a piece of paper. "Abductin' yore pore old uncle! Aimin' to hold him for ransom! It's all writ down in yore own handwritin' right here on this-here paper! Sayin' yo're takin' Jacob away off into the mountains--warnin' me not to try to foller! Same as threatenin' me! I never heered of such doin's! Soon as that good-for-nothin' Joe Hopkins brung me that there insolent letter, I went right after the sheriff.... Joshua Braxton, what air you doin' in them ondecent togs? My land, I dunno what we're comin' to! Well, sheriff, what you standin' there for like a ninny? Why'n't you put some handcuffs and chains and shackles on him? Air you skeered of the big lunkhead?"

"Aw, heck," I said. "This is all a mistake. I warn't threatenin' nobody in that there letter--"

"Then where's Jacob?" she demanded. "Prejuice him imejitately, or--"

"He ducked into that cave," said Glanton.

I stuck my head in and roared: "Uncle Jacob! You come outa there and explain before I come in after you!"

He snuck out looking meek and down-trodden, and I says: "You tell these idjits that I ain't no kidnaper."

"That's right," he said. "I brung him along with me."

"Hell!" said the sheriff, disgustedly. "Have we come all this way on a wild goose chase? I should of knew better'n to listen to a woman--"

"You shet yore fool mouth!" squalled Aunt Lavaca. "A fine sheriff you be. Anyway--what was Breckinridge doin' up here with you, Jacob?"

"He was helpin' me look for a mine, Lavacky," he said.

"Helpin' you?" she screeched. "Why, I sent him to fetch you back! Breckinridge Elkins, I'll tell yore pap about this, you big, lazy, good-for-nothin', low-down, ornery--"

"Aw, shet up!" I roared, exasperated beyond endurance. I seldom lets my voice go its full blast. Echoes rolled through the canyon like thunder, the trees shook and the pine cones fell like hail, and rocks tumbled down the mountainsides. Aunt Lavaca staggered backwards with a outraged squall.

"Jacob!" she hollered. "Air you goin' to 'low that ruffian to use that-there tone of voice to me? I demands that you flail the livin' daylights outa the scoundrel right now!"

Uncle Jacob winked at me.

"Now, now, Lavacky," he started soothing her, and she give him a clip under the ear that changed ends with him. The sheriff and his posse and Van Brock took out up the ravine like the devil was after 'em, and Glanton bit off a chaw of tobaccer and says to me, he says: "Well, what was you fixin' to say about women's gentle sweetness?"

"Nothin'," I snarled. "Come on, let's git goin'. I yearns to find a more quiet and secluded spot than this-here'n. I'm stayin' with Joshua and you and the grizzly."